KU-243-887

ALEX'S Outing

Mary Dickinson

Illustrated by
Charlotte Firmin

Hippo

Scholastic Children's Books,
Commonwealth House, 1-19 New Oxford Street,
London WC1A 1NU, UK
a division of Scholastic Ltd
London ~ New York ~ Toronto ~ Sydney ~ Auckland

First published in hardback by André Deutsch Limited, 1983
Published by Scholastic Publications Ltd, 1994
Reissued by Scholastic Ltd, 1996

Text copyright © Mary Dickinson, 1983
Illustrations copyright © Charlotte Firmin, 1983

ISBN: 0 590 13421 3

Printed in Belgium by Proost International

All rights reserved

10 9 8 7 6 5 4 3

The right of Mary Dickinson and Charlotte Firmin to be identified as the
author and illustrator of this work respectively has been asserted by them in
accordance with the Copyright, Designs and Patents Act, 1988.

This book is sold subject to the condition that it shall not, by way of trade or
otherwise, be lent, resold, hired out, or otherwise circulated without the
publisher's prior consent in any form of binding other than that in
which it is published and without a similar condition, including this
condition, being imposed upon the subsequent purchaser.

"We're going to the countree
the countreee
the countreeeeee," shouted Alex and
Roy and Bernice and Barnie and Greg and Wendy
as they waited for the bus to come.

"Stop that terrible noise," said Wendy's
mother. "Wendy, come and stand with me."
"I think it's meant to be singing," said
Alex's mother.
"They're very excited about the outing,"
said Barnie's mother.
Just then the bus arrived.

The mothers sat at the front of the bus.
The children rushed to the back.
There they bounced up and down on the springy seats all the way to the country.
Wendy had a lovely time.
Her mother kept saying, "Be quiet." But nobody seemed to hear.

"This is where you lot get off," shouted
the driver.
Everyone got off.
All around them the country looked very
smooth and green.
It made Alex want to run. Run as fast as
he could.
"Beat you to the trees," he cried, and before
the mothers could shout stop, the children
were running away.
"They'll get lost," said Wendy's mother.
"Don't worry," said Alex's mother. "They
won't go far."

It wasn't long before Alex stopped.
His tummy hurt and his feet felt very heavy.
Suddenly he felt frightened. He was all alone in the country.
He tried to turn back, but his feet wouldn't move.
"Help," cried Alex. "I'm stuck in the mud!"

Roy and Greg came and pulled him out.
There was a lot of slipping and splashing
and Alex fell over.
"You're very muddy," said Wendy.
"I get told off if I get dirty."
"Well, I don't," said Alex crossly.

"Children," called the mothers, "come and look at the cow."
"I don't like cows," said Alex, and he mooed as loudly as he could at the cow.

The cow didn't move, but there was a squelchy thundering noise, and a whole herd of cows came galloping up and breathed over Alex.

"I think they like you," said his mother.

"Aren't they big?" said Bernice.

"Oh, do be careful, Wendy," said her mother, "they might splash you."

"Come on, it's time to eat," said Alex's mother, walking away.

"I'm not hungry," complained Alex.

But everyone else was.

While the others ate, Alex swung about in
the trees.
"Look Mum, look at me," he shouted.
But Alex's mother didn't look. She was
too busy talking to Barnie's mother.
There was a ripping sound.
"Oh, Alex," whispered Wendy. "You've torn
your jeans. Bet your mother will be cross."
"No," said Alex, "she didn't see."

Alex decided it was time he had lunch.
He ate all his lunch and lots of
everybody else's.

After lunch the mothers picked blackberries. Alex felt too full to eat any, so he put some in his pocket for later. Then he crept among the bushes with Roy, trying to frighten Wendy. "Stop it!" said Wendy, throwing blackberries at Alex. "You're just stupid and messy." "Hee! Hee!" laughed Alex. "You've got purple from the blackberries all over you. Bet your mother will be cross!" "Oh, dear," said Wendy sadly.

When it was time to go home, Alex sat with his mother.
She was *still* talking to Barnie's mother.
In the seat behind, Wendy's mother was wiping Wendy's face and telling her off.
Poor Wendy, thought Alex.

On the way home from the bus stop, Alex's mother showed him the blackberries she had picked.

Alex remembered the ones in his pocket.

He slid in his hand.

Ugh.

His pocket was all wet and sticky. The blackberries were very squashed. There was a big patch of purple on his jeans.

Will Mum be cross? wondered Alex.

When they got home Alex went straight into the bathroom, took off his clothes and hid them in the dirty clothes basket.

"What are you up to?" asked his mother.

"I fancy a bath," said Alex.

Alex's mother looked surprised.

"You usually hate baths. Quick, let's get you in before you change your mind."

When Alex was in the bath, his mother
found his clothes.
Alex waited. Was she going to be cross?

"What a mess," said Alex's mother loudly.
But then she looked at Alex and smiled.
"I suppose I should have guessed. I don't
mind; it was such a lovely outing."